For Holden and Riley

Sometimes in life you're the dinkleface, and sometimes you'll find yourself looking at him. Whichever side you're on, stay strong.

Doing the right thing is not always popular.
But it is always the right choice.

I love you always.

© 2018 James P. Halpin III

Big Butt Dinkleface

A tale of bullying, bravery and weaponized flatulence

Story by James Halpin   Illustrated by Tanja Russita

There once was a lonely
boy, caring and kind,

Who tried very hard
for a friend he might find.

But the bullies just laughed,
calling him a disgrace.

He was known at his school
as Big Butt Dinkleface.

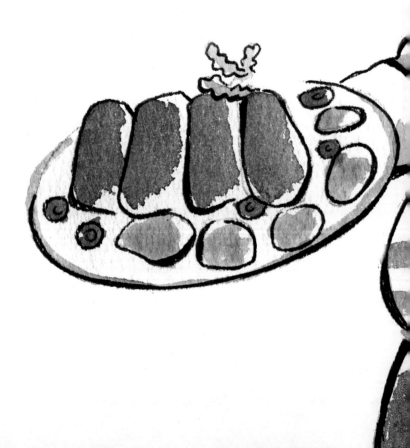

A nice boy was he,
always wanting to play.

But the other kids
constantly sent him away.

For Big Butt Dinkleface
was different than most.

He had a butt
twice as big
as a Sunday
pot roast.

But it wasn't just big;
it was loud and explosive.

His farts could peel paint
like an acid corrosive.

And the smell — oh the
smell was just terribly toxic.

Anybody who sniffed it
would beg him to stop it.

And so it went that,
day after day,

Poor Dinkleface had
no way he could play.

At recess he sat
all alone in a tree,

While the others played games,
happy as could be.

5

Then, one day, something
terrible happened at school.

Three robbers burst in and
said, "Give us your jewels!"

All the kids on the playground
jumped up, ran away.

Those trapped in the school
had no choice but to stay.

Dinkleface watched
from his perch in the tree.

Then he took a deep breath
and said, "I'll set them free."

Calling on all of the
courage he could muster,

He marched to the building,
perhaps like old Custer.

He burst in the school,
going through the front door,

And staring at the robbers,
he shouted, "No more!"

He turned around,
aiming his butt at their heads.

His eyes began straining;
his face grew quite red.

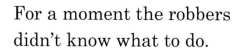

For a moment the robbers
didn't know what to do.

Then they laughed and
they said, "Now we'll rob
you, boy, too!"

At the very same moment
they pulled out their guns,

Dinkleface bombed them —
five megatons.

12

The sound shook the walls
and shattered the windows.

The robbers were dazed
by the battering wind flow.

But then, when the shock
wave had settled at last,

The robbers were hit
with the smell of the gas.

The smell was quite wretched
and perfectly gross.

It made each of them puke
just a bit in the throat.

The stench was so nasty
and foul to smell,

And so powerful that
it rang alarm bells.

The smell was so awful
it's hard to describe.
But in the name of science,
let's give it a try.

It was something like
rotting eggs left in the sun;
or maybe a pond that's been
drained, leaving scum.

That's not quite right;
no, it was more like manure,
a pile from ten thousand
cows, perhaps more.

15

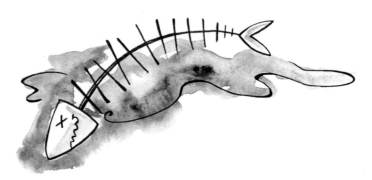

Or maybe 'twas more like the smell of dead fish
that were left out too long and have started to squish.

The smell of a garbage truck might be a match,
if it's hot out and flies are all swarming the trash.

Perhaps, though, the smell
could best be described,

As a smell so rancid
that vile vultures cried.

However you describe it,
the effect was the same.

The robbers were going
quite out of their brains.

Their faces all turned
different colors of green,

As they stumbled 'round
seeking air that was clean.

When they finally found
their way to the outside,

They had tears in their eyes
that made them go blind.

In their rush to get out
they smacked into a tree,

And they fell to the ground
in a pile, all three.

The robbers were left
feeling most unwell,

As they were loaded up
and taken to a holding cell.

Then all the kids ran
to Big Butt Dinkleface,

And they said,
"Hey, that butt of yours
actually is great."

They hoisted him up to
ride on their shoulders,

With the weight of his
rear pushing down,
like big boulders.

They cheered and they shouted and formed a parade.
"Dinkleface just saved the day! Hooray!"
The principal came out and thanked him sincerely,
For being so brave to risk death, quite nearly.

So although his butt
was stunningly vast,

And loud and disgusting
when he let out a blast,

Dinkleface gained
many friends on that day.

And from then on the kids
always asked him to play.

But now when they call him
to join in their games,

They no longer use
that mean-spirited name.

Never again was he
Big Butt Dinkleface.

Now, he's known simply
as little Bobby Chase.

About the author:

James Halpin is an award-winning reporter who has worked as a journalist for more than a decade. He is a graduate of the University of Alaska Anchorage and has worked at several daily newspapers, mostly covering crime and courts. Prior to becoming a journalist, Halpin served in the U.S. Marine Corps in Okinawa, Japan, and at Camp Lejeune, N.C. He resides in Mountain Top, Pa., with his wife and two children.

About the illustrator:

Tanja Russita is a book illustrator living in Sweden with her husband and two kids — who are a never-ending source of inspiration and, simultaneously, a black hole that is always competing for her time. Hiking, nature and playing the guitar in the company of friends are three things that make her especially happy. And happiness is essential for drawing!

34794590R00020

Made in the USA
San Bernardino, CA
04 May 2019